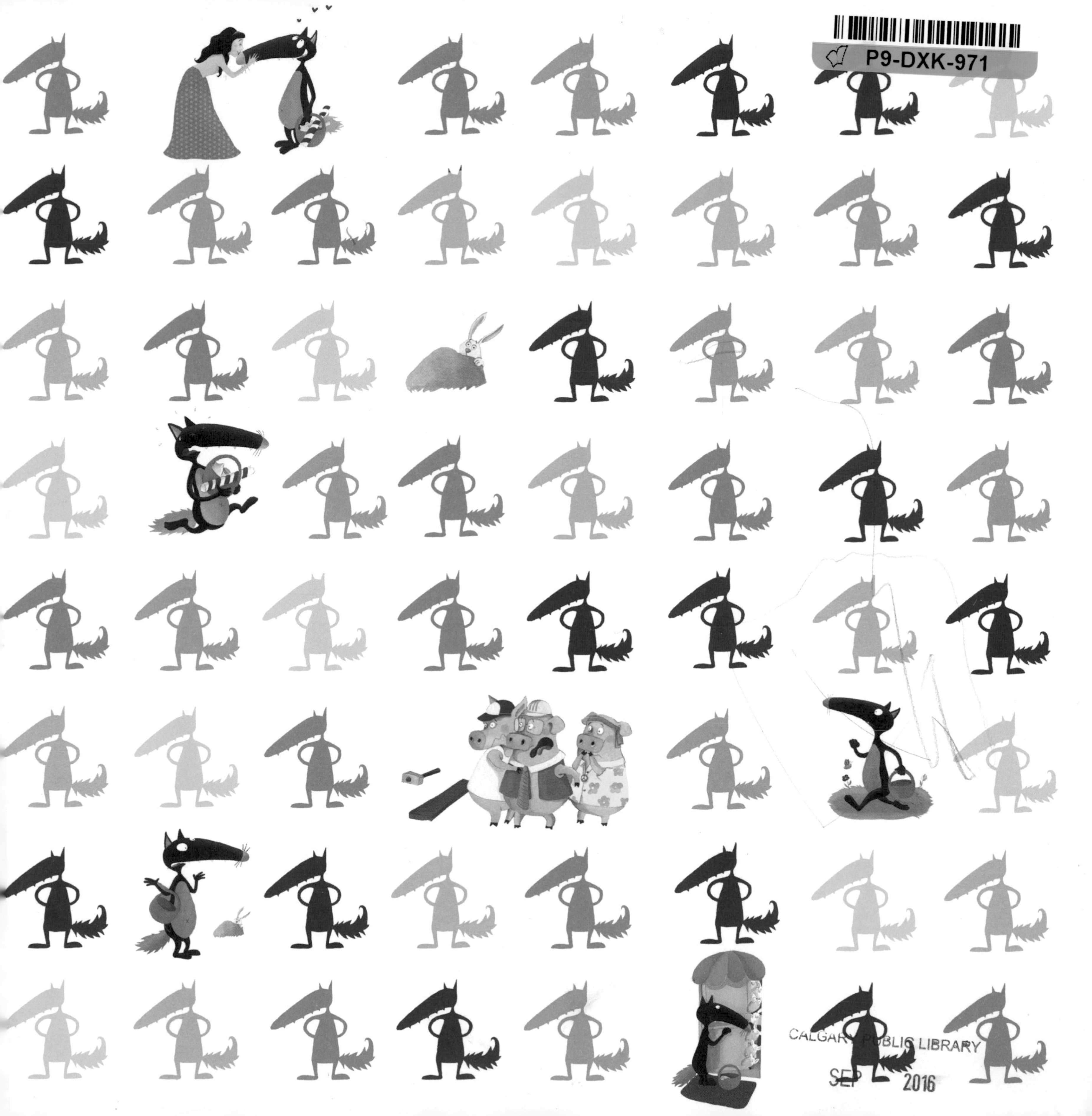

To Fairy Tales, past and present, from here, there and everywhere...
and to their authors who have so often delighted me...
OL

To all the little piglets, chicks, kids and other small creatures
who are still afraid of the Big Bad Wolf...
ET